BLACK PANTHER

A NATION UNDER OUR FEET: PART 4

MARVEL

ABDOBOOKS.COM

Reinforced library bound edition published in 2020 by Spotlight,
a division of ABDO, PO Box 398166, Minneapolis, Minnesota 55439.
Spotlight produces high-quality reinforced library bound editions for
schools and libraries. Published by agreement with Marvel Characters, Inc.

Printed in the United States of America, North Mankato, Minnesota.
042019
092019

Library of Congress Control Number: 2018965952

Publisher's Cataloging-in-Publication Data

Names: Coates, Ta-Nehisi, author. | Stelfreeze, Brian; Martin, Laura; Sprouse, Chris; Story, Karl, illustrators.
Title: A nation under our feet / writer: Ta-Nehisi Coates; art: Brian Stelfreeze ; Laura Martin ; Chris Sprouse ; Karl Story.
Description: Minneapolis, Minnesota : Spotlight, 2020 | Series: Black Panther
Summary: With a dramatic upheaval in Wakanda on the horizon, T'Challa knows his kingdom needs to change to survive, but he struggles to find balance in his roles as king and the Black Panther.
Identifiers: ISBN 9781532143519 (pt. 1 ; lib. bdg.) | ISBN 9781532143526 (pt. 2 ; lib. bdg.) | ISBN 9781532143533 (pt. 3 ; lib. bdg.) | ISBN 9781532143540 (pt. 4 ; lib. bdg.) | ISBN 9781532143557 (pt. 5 ; lib. bdg.) | ISBN 9781532143564 (pt. 6 ; lib. bdg.)
Subjects: LCSH: Black Panther (Fictitious character)--Juvenile fiction. | Superheroes--Juvenile fiction. | Kings and rulers--Juvenile fiction. | Graphic novels--Juvenile fiction. | T'Challa, of Wakanda (Fictitious character)--Juvenile fiction.
Classification: DDC 741.5--dc23

Spotlight

A Division of ABDO
abdobooks.com

BLACK PANTHER

T'CHALLA TRACKED THE GROUP OF REBELS KNOWN AS **THE PEOPLE** TO THE NIGANDAN BORDER AND WAS ABLE TO STRIKE DOWN ONE OF THEIR LEADERS, **ZENZI**, BEFORE SHE COULD USE HER MIND POWERS ON HIM AGAIN.

BEFORE T'CHALLA'S SECRET POLICE, THE **HATUT ZERAZE**, COULD ARREST THEM, REBEL LEADER **TETU** USED HIS POWER OVER NATURE TO ESCAPE WITH THE COMATOSE ZENZI.

MEANWHILE, **AYO** AND **ANEKA** -- FORMERLY OF THE **DORA MILAJE**, NOW KNOWN AS THE **MIDNIGHT ANGELS** -- ARE LIBERATING OPPRESSED WAKANDANS THAT THE CROWN HAS NEGLECTED FOR TOO LONG.

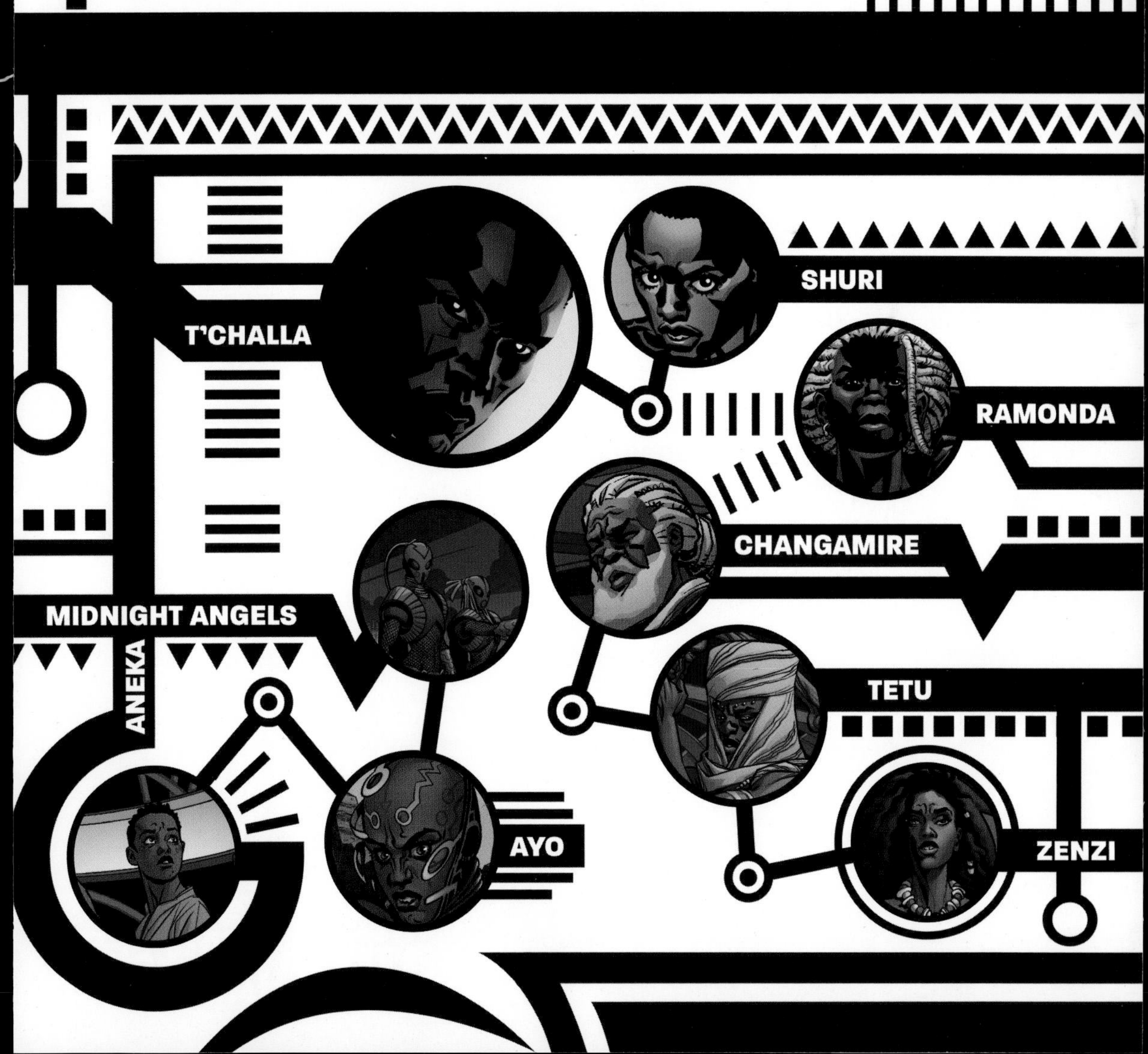

A NATION UNDER OUR FEET
part 4
writer TA-NEHISI COATES
artist BRIAN STELFREEZE
color artists LAURA MARTIN
with MATT M
letterer VC's JOE SABINO
design MANNY MEDEROS
logo RIAN HUGHES
cover by BRIAN STELFREEZE
and LAURA MARTIN
variant covers by
SANFORD GREENE
DAVID YARDIN
assistant editor CHRIS ROBINSON
editor WIL MOSS
executive editor TOM BREVOORT
editor in chief AXEL ALONSO chief creative officer JOE QUESADA
publisher DAN BUCKLEY executive producer ALAN FINE
BLACK PANTHER created by
STAN LEE &
JACK KIRBY

KING T'CHALLA, OUR RECENT OPERATION NEUTRALIZED THIS *ZENZI*, THIS *"REVEALER."* TURMOIL IN THE REGION OF THE GREAT MOUND HAS WITHERED.
OUR OPERATIVES REPORT SOME SUBVERSIVE ACTIVITY ALONG THE NIGANDAN FRONTIER, BUT THE EASTERN REGION HAS CALMED. *THAT IS THE GOOD NEWS.*
MENA NGAI
ZENZI AND HER MEN ESCAPED. ANY *"GOOD NEWS"* MUST BE TAKEN AS A PAUSE IN THE ACTION.
INDEED, MY SON. THE DAMAGE DONE BY OUR *"INCIDENT"* AT THE GREAT MOUND WAS PROFOUND. IT MAY BE IMPERCEPTIBLE AT THE MOMENT, BUT IT HAS NOT VANISHED.
HODARI, WHAT CAN YOU TELL US OF THE SHAMAN?
BIRNIN BASHENGA
MENA NGAI

WE ARE STILL WORKING ON IT. WE HAVE A NAME-- *TETU*. WE KNOW HE WAS ONCE A PUPIL AT HEKIMA SHULÉ.
CHANGAMIRE.

WHO?
CHANGAMIRE, A DISSIDENT PHILOSOPHER AT THE SHULÉ. AND BEFORE THAT...

...THE HANDPICKED TUTOR FOR KING T'CHAKA'S ROYAL COURT.
AND WHAT HAPPENED?
KING T'CHAKA EXILED HIM FOR EXHORTATION AGAINST THE MONARCHY.

HODARI, DO YOU HAVE ANYTHING SOLID CONNECTING CHANGAMIRE AND THE SHAMAN?

ONLY THIS.

THAT IS NOT ENOUGH.
BUT IT MAY WARRANT A VISIT, MY KING.
PERHAPS, AKILI. BUT BY SOMEONE WITH A LIGHTER TOUCH THAN THE *HATUT ZERAZE*.

HODARI, LISTEN, I UNDERSTAND THAT YOU HAVE BEEN TASKED WITH THE IMPOSSIBLE. YOUR OPERATIVES HAVE BEEN DIMINISHED. OUR NETWORK IS THREADBARE.
BUT I NEED THIS. YOUR PEOPLE NEED THIS. FIND THIS TETU. FIND THE REVEALER. UNCOVER ALL THEIR CONNECTIONS. FOR THE GOOD OF THE COUNTRY, YOU MUST DO THIS.
ON MY WORD, KING T'CHALLA.

NOW, WHAT IS THE **BAD** NEWS?

FOR WEEKS WE HAVE HEARD DISTURBING RUMORS OUT OF THE NORTH. WE LACKED CONFIRMATION UNTIL LAST NIGHT, WHEN AN OPERATIVE IN THE CRYSTAL FOREST SENT US THIS FOOTAGE.
M'BAKU ONCE HELD SWAY HERE. BUT AFTER HE WAS KILLED, HIS YOUNGER BROTHER, MANDLA, TOOK UP THE MAN-APE MANTLE AND CONSOLIDATED POWER.

"THAT WAS THE STATE OF THINGS UNTIL SOMETIME LAST MONTH. WE DO NOT KNOW HOW IT HAPPENED. BUT THIS ONE, ON THE RIGHT, IS WELL KNOWN TO US--ANEKA, A RENEGADE CAPTAIN OF THE DORA MILAJE, SENTENCED TO DEATH FOR ASSASSINATION.

"THE ONE ON THE LEFT, AYO, ANOTHER OF OUR ADORED ONES, EVIDENTLY STOLE TWO OF OUR ARMOR PROTOTYPES AND USED THEM TO FREE ANEKA. THEY HAVE BEEN MARAUDING THROUGH THE COUNTRY EVER SINCE.

"WE HAVE BEEN PURSUING THEM FOR SOME TIME, BUT OUR FORCES HAVE BEEN SO DEPLETED, OUR NEEDS SO VAST, THAT WE LOST TRACK OF THEM.
"FORGIVE ME, MY KING...

"...BUT THAT WAS A MISTAKE.

"THESE RENEGADES OVERRAN MANDLA'S FORCES...

"...RAZED THE CITADEL OF THE JABARI FOREFATHERS...

"...AND CONVENED TRIBUNALS."

THE JABARI TRIBESMEN AND SEVERAL *DORA MILAJE* HAVE SIDED WITH ANEKA AND AYO. THEY HAVE BEGUN ASSEMBLING COMMUNES, CALLING FOR ELECTIONS, WRITING AND ENFORCING LAWS...
...MY KING, THIS IS NOT MERE HOOLIGANISM...

...THIS IS REVOLUTION.

IT CERTAINLY IS NOT THAT I AM DISHONORED OR EVEN DISPLEASED BY YOUR PRESENCE. AND YET I CANNOT ESCAPE THE FEELING THAT...

AZZARIA, THE LEARNED CITY
...YOU ARE SOMEHOW DISPLEASED WITH ME, QUEEN MOTHER.

WHY CHANGAMIRE, CAN TWO FRIENDS NOT SPEAK OF THE DAYS WHEN THEY WERE YOUNG TOGETHER?

TWO FRIENDS CAN AND SHOULD, QUEEN MOTHER. BUT WE APPEAR TO BE PRESENTLY MORE THAN TWO.

AS YOU WISH.

BETTER NOW?
YES.

NOW TELL ME WHAT YOU WANT. HAVE I VIOLATED SOME EDICT BY SPEAKING TO MY PUPILS AS ADULTS? AM I TO BE EXILED FROM WAKANDA ENTIRELY?
SO THE FIRE STILL BURNS, OLD FRIEND.
DON'T CONDESCEND TO ME, RAMONDA. I AM NOT ONE OF YOUR PETS. I GAVE THAT UP YEARS AGO, RIGHT WHEN I GAVE UP ON *YOU*.

SO YOU DID.
ONCE, I REGRETTED THAT. I WAS YOUNG, IN A STRANGE LAND, AND MADE BY YOU TO FULLY FEEL LIKE A WOMAN.

AND THEN I REMEMBERED THAT MY DESTINY WAS NOT TO BE A WOMAN, BUT TO BE A *QUEEN*.

THERE WAS NO CHOICE, CHANGAMIRE.
THERE IS NEVER ANY CHOICE FOR ANYONE HERE. WAKANDA IS SCIENCE AND WONDER, ALL OF IT ACHIEVED BY ENSURING YOUR SUBJECTS DO NOT ASK TOO MANY QUESTIONS.
WAKANDA HAS ALL THE INTELLIGENCE ANY ADVANCED SOCIETY WOULD WANT, AND NONE OF THE WISDOM THAT ANY FREE SOCIETY NEEDS.
PERHAPS THAT IS CHANGING. HAVE YOU NOT HEARD? YOUR GLORIOUS AND ROMANTIC REVOLUTION IS FINALLY UPON US.
THERE IS NOTHING GLORIOUS IN MASSACRING YOUR OWN PEOPLE.
I AGREE. AS DOES OUR KING. AS DO WE ALL. OUR MEN AT THE MOUND THAT DAY WERE NOT THEMSELVES. SOMEONE ELSE WAS INFLUENCING THEM. PERHAPS YOU MIGHT KNOW WHO.
YOU ARE MISTAKEN.
TELL ME: HOW, PRECISELY, AM I MISTAKEN?
NO. I WILL NOT DO THE WORK OF YOUR AGENTS. I WON'T ENROLL IN YOUR NATIONAL LIE.
IT IS A LIE--ONE THAT MAKES YOUR LIFE OF PHILOSOPHY POSSIBLE. WE STUDIED A LOT TOGETHER. AND YET IN ALL OUR TIME WE NEVER STUDIED A SINGLE NATION FOUNDED ON TRUTH AND CANDOR.
MY TEACHERS WERE IMAGINATIVE AND VISIONARY. BUT THEY DUG NO WELLS, BUILT NO WALLS, FED NO CHILDREN. THE BEST OF THEM WERE ONLY MEN OF THEORY.
BUT WE WERE WAKANDA. WE WERE THE GOLDEN CITY. WE WERE SUPPOSED TO BE EXCEPTIONAL.
WE STILL ARE WAKANDA. AND WE WILL ALWAYS BE EXCEPTIONAL. YOU DID NOT CONDEMN US FOR BEING MEDIOCRE. YOU CONDEMNED US FOR NOT BEING DIVINE.
AND CHANGAMIRE, I THOUGHT YOU WERE MANY THINGS, BUT I NEVER THOUGHT YOU WERE ANYONE'S PET.
KEEP YOUR HEAD DOWN, OLD FRIEND. THE STORM IS COMING.
"IT WAS THE QUESTIONS THAT BROUGHT ME TO THE SHULE.

"AND THE QUESTIONS THAT FORCED ME TO LEAVE.

"I SOUGHT ANSWERS THAT MOCKED THE MEAN PHYSICS OF MEN AND ULTIMATELY LAY IN THE DEEPER NATURE OF ALL LIVING THINGS.

"BUT WHEN I SEARCHED, I FOUND ONLY CHARLATANS DELUDING THE COMMON MAN WITH SUPERSTITION AND HOAXES.

"I RETREATED DEEPER INTO THE WILDERNESS OF WAKANDA. I FOLLOWED NO MAN, BUT TOOK WISDOM FROM ROOT, BARK, AND EARTH.

"I RETURNED WITH ANSWERS.

"AND FROM THE ANSWERS I DREW THE POWER TO PUNISH THE ACQUISITIVE, WHO WOULD TAKE FROM THE LITTLE PEOPLE EVEN OUR SHARE OF DAYLIGHT, IF THEY COULD."

I WANTED A NEW COUNTRY, A COUNTRY THAT RESPECTED ALL OF US EQUALLY, AND RESPECTED THE EARTH FROM WHICH WE ALL HAIL, AND THE EARTH TO WHICH WE ALL SHALL RETURN.

I BELIEVE I HAVE FOUND THAT COUNTRY.

I COME TO OFFER YOU MY ADMIRATION. TOPPLING THE JABARI TYRANT WAS A GREAT SERVICE TO THE NATION. BUT MORE, I OFFER YOU MY ARMS. IT WILL NOT END WITH THE JABARI. *WAR* IS COMING.

TETU, EACH DAY ANOTHER OF OUR SISTERS JOINS THE CAUSE. EACH DAY WE GROW STRONGER.

THE MIDNIGHT ANGELS WERE ENOUGH FOR MANDLA. THEY WILL BE ENOUGH FOR *DAMISA-SARKI* TOO.

BUT CAN YOU BE SURE IT WILL BE HARAMU-FAL ALONE? WHAT OF HIS ALLIES BEYOND WAKANDA? WHAT OF THIS WIND-RIDER? WHAT OF THE LADY OF LIGHT?
WE ARE NOT ARRAYED MERELY AGAINST TYRANNY, BUT AGAINST A PARTICULAR DISHONOR. TO MASSACRE YOUR OWN PEOPLE, TO BRAZENLY ASSAULT A CAMP OF OLD WOMEN AND CHILDREN...
WE ARE NOT BLIND TO RECENT EVENTS, TETU. NOR ARE WE BLIND TO DAMISA-SARKI'S ALLIES.
BUT WE ARE, AS YOU SAY, A NEW COUNTRY, A NEW NATION. PRUDENCE IS REQUIRED.
EVEN IN YOUR ALLIES.
ESPECIALLY IN OUR ALLIES.
WE KNOW WHO YOU ARE. WE KNOW OF YOUR BATTLES WITH THE KING. WE THINK YOU MAY WELL PROVE TO BE A TRUE FRIEND OF OUR CAUSE.
BUT RIGHT NOW ALL WE SHARE ARE KIND WORDS AND A COMMON ENEMY. THAT IS NOT YET ENOUGH.

CHANGAMIRE DID NOT TELL ME ANYTHING. HE DID NOT WANT TO. BUT EVEN IF HE HAD WANTED TO, HE HAD NOTHING TO TELL.
HOW CAN YOU BE SURE?
BECAUSE I KNOW HIM.

"WHEN I FIRST CAME TO WAKANDA, IT WAS A FASHIONABLE TIME. THE ENTIRE COURT WAS IN THE THRALL OF PHILOSOPHY. IT WAS BELIEVED THAT OUR ADVANCED SOCIETY NEEDED TO DEVELOP AN ADVANCED MORALITY.

"YOU KNOW YOUR FATHER AS A WARRIOR, AND HE WAS THAT, BUT HE WAS ALSO AN ENLIGHTENED MAN. HE INVITED THE SEERS INTO THE COURT. YOUR FATHER BELIEVED IN A NEW AGE. BUT THE CONSTANT WARS KILLED HIS FAITH."

I SUSPECT YOU KNOW THE REST. WHAT I *WILL* TELL YOU IS THAT CHANGAMIRE WAS THE MOST HONORABLE OF THAT LOT. HE WAS A TUTOR TO ME PERSONALLY IN WAKANDAN PHILOSOPHY AND ITS POSSIBLE EVOLUTION.

I GRANT YOU WE HAVE NOT BEEN IN CONSTANT CONTACT SINCE THE OLD DAYS, BUT CHANGAMIRE IS NOT A REVOLUTIONARY. HE RENOUNCED VIOLENCE.
AND YET HERE WE ARE.

INDEED. MAKE OF CHANGAMIRE WHAT YOU WILL. YOU REQUESTED MY COUNSEL AND MY INTELLIGENCE. I HAVE OFFERED IT.
AND IF I ACCEPT YOUR INTELLIGENCE, WHAT IS YOUR COUNSEL NOW, MOTHER?

I DO NOT THINK YOUR PROBLEM IS AN OLD PHILOSOPHER.

I DO NOT THINK YOUR PROBLEM IS THE RENEGADE *DORA MILAJE.*
YOUR PROBLEM, T'CHALLA...

...IS THE PEOPLE.

WHAT YOUR FATHER UNDERSTOOD, BUT CHANGAMIRE NEVER DID, WAS THAT THE FIRST RULE OF ANY GOVERNMENT WAS TO SAFEGUARD THE PEOPLE.

WE HAVE FAILED AT THAT--DOOM, NAMOR, THE BLACK ORDER, AND THREATS THAT ARE NOT EVEN KNOWN TO THEM.
BUT THERE IS MORE.

WHAT *CHANGAMIRE* UNDERSTOOD, AND YOUR FATHER ULTIMATELY DID NOT, IS THAT PROTECTION IS NOT ENOUGH. FORCE IS NOT ENOUGH.

TO WHAT END DOES ALL OUR WEAPONRY ANGLE US? WHAT ARE WE REALLY PROTECTING? OUR LIVES ARE NOT ENOUGH. WHAT DO OUR LIVES MEAN?
ARE YOU REALLY ASKING ME THIS, MOTHER? WE ARE PROTECTING OUR HERITAGE, OUR TRADITIONS.
YOU ARE SMARTER THAN THAT, T'CHALLA...THE PEOPLE KNOW THIS STORY WELL. YOU ARE GOING TO HAVE TO GIVE THEM MORE.

FOR MY PEOPLE, I HAVE BATTLED WORLD-BREAKERS, DEATH CULTISTS, AND MEN WHO WOULD MAKE THEMSELVES GODS. FOR MY PEOPLE, I LOST THE ONLY WOMAN I EVER TRULY LOVED.
THERE IS NOTHING LEFT, MOTHER. I HAVE GIVEN IT ALL.

NO, T'CHALLA. LET US NOT MINCE WORDS HERE--YOU HAVE NEVER GIVEN WILLINGLY. YOU FEEL THE WEIGHT OF THE CROWN, BUT YOU HAVE NEVER FELT THE GREAT HONOR OF BEING KING. YOUR PEOPLE ARE A BURDEN TO YOU, AND YOU HAVE NEVER LET THEM FORGET THIS.
YOU SAY YOU HAVE GIVEN IT ALL. YOU ARE WRONG. YOU HAVE NEVER *TRULY* GIVEN YOURSELF TO YOUR COUNTRY.

"HOW AM I TO DO THIS, MOTHER?"
"BY GIVING THOSE WHO LOVE YOU SOMETHING MORE THAN RECITATION AND CEREMONY. BY GIVING THAT WHICH ALL GREAT KINGS ULTIMATELY OFFER...
"INSPIRATION."

NOW. WHERE WERE WE?
THE MATH, OF COURSE. WHAT ELSE IS THERE, TETU?
YES. THE MATH.
LIKE I WAS SAYING, A GUY CAN ONLY MASTER SO MUCH, AND AFTER PARTICLE PHYSICS, NANOTECH, AND BIOMECHATRONICS, I ADMIT, I KIND OF TAPPED OUT.

BUT NEVER LET IT BE SAID THAT *ZEKE STANE* COULDN'T COUNT. AND IT SEEMS TO ME, WITHOUT THAT NIGANDAN BIRD, THE SCORE IS SOMETHING LIKE T'CHALLA, 1,000-- YOU, ZERO.

YOU'RE DOWN, BUDDY. AND THEY'RE OUT THERE FLAUNTING IT.

RUBBING YOUR NOSE IN IT. GLOATING.

THE SITUATION IS INDEED PRECARIOUS.
PRECARIOUS DON'T EVEN COVER IT, FRIEND. WITHOUT A MAJOR UPGRADE, T'CHALLA IS GOING TO DRAW AND QUARTER YOU, THEN PUT YOUR HEAD ON A PIKE.
IT IS NOT FEAR OF MY DEATH THAT BRINGS US TOGETHER, EZEKIEL STANE. IT IS FEAR OF *LOSING*. FEAR OF TYRANNY EXTENDING ITSELF, UNCHALLENGED, EVEN ONE MORE DAY.
HAVE YOU EVER ACTUALLY SEEN SOMEONE DRAWN AND QUARTERED? OKAY, HERE'S THE THING...

"...YOU SAY YOU WANT A REVOLUTION, BUT ARE YOU READY FOR THE FUTURE, FRIEND?
"LET ME TELL YOU WHAT IS COMING.
"PANIC IN THE STREETS.
"FIRE IN THE SKY.
"CASUALTIES.
"AGONY."

"THE CASUALTIES, KING T'CHALLA, WERE EXTENSIVE. BOTH THE INJURED...
"...AND THE DEAD."

IF NOT FOR THE SHIELDING FROM YOUR VIBRANIUM SUIT, OUR QUEEN-MOTHER WOULD HAVE BEEN AMONG THEM. HER INJURIES ARE EXTENSIVE. BUT SHE WILL LIVE.
THANK YOU, HODARI. NOW, ALL OF YOU, LISTEN: NO MORE DISCOURSE. NO MORE DELIBERATION. NO MORE EXCUSES.
NO MORE MERCY.
WE KNOW WHAT THIS IS. IT IS WAR, AND WAR IS OUR NATION'S TRADE.
IT HAS BEEN SO FOR GENERATIONS. WE ARE WAKANDA. WE WILL NOT BE TERRORIZED.
WE ARE TERROR ITSELF.
TO BE CONTINUED